This book belongs to

....

Quarto is the authority on a wide range of topics.

Quarto educates, entertains and enriches the lives of our readers—enthusiasts and lovers of hands-on living.

www.quartoknows.com

© 2019 Quarto Publishing plc

First published in 2019 by QED Publishing,
an imprint of The Quarto Group.
The Old Brewery, 6 Blundell Street,
London N7 9BH, United Kingdom.
T (0)20 7700 6700 F (0)20 7700 8066
www.QuartoKnows.com

A catalogue record for this book is available from the British Library.

ISBN 978-1-78603-606-3

Based on the original story by Peter Bently and Duncan Beedle

Author of adapted text: Katie Woolley
Series Editor: Joyce Bentley
Series Designer: Sarah Peden

Manufactured in Dongguan, China TL112018

9 8 7 6 5 4 3 2 1

MIX
Paper from
responsible sources
FSC® C104723

Reading Gems

Pem's Snack

Focus sounds in this book

a
sat

b
bugs

c
can

ck
snack

d
Nid

e
Pem

g
Gop

h
ha

i
sit

k
kick

m
Pem

n
San

o
Gop

p
up

r
rocket

s
sat

t
tips

u
up

The bugs sit in Pem's big rocket.

It can go up.

The bugs go to the big rock.

The bugs go to get a snack.

No snack.

No snack.

10

Is it a snack?

No snack!

Ah! A big snack!

Pem, Gop and San run to get it.

Pem has got the snack.
Kick! The snack tips.

Nid got it!

Num, num.

Nid got up. Nid had sat on Pem's rocket.

Pem is sad.

But the bugs can get it back.

The bugs get bits and bobs.

Ta da! The rocket is back!

Pem, Gop and San get into the rocket.

The rocket can go up!

And Pem can get a snack!

25

Let's Talk About Pem's Snack

Look at the back cover.

Point to the focus letters.

Can you make the letter sounds?

Can you find the tricky word 'go' in the story?

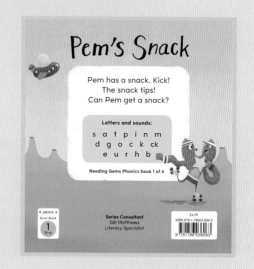

Point to the the letter 'i' in the middle of the word 'sit'.

What sound does 'i' make?

Can you find some other words in the story with the letter 'i' in them?

Can you think of any other words with 'i' in them?

Find the letter 's' at the beginning of San's name.

Can you sound out the whole name?

Can you read all the other bugs' names?

Why was Pem sad?

How did the bugs make him feel better?

What did the bugs do at the end of the story?

Did you like the story about Pem's snack?

What was your favourite bit?

Fun and Games

What sound does each pair begin with?
Can you think of another word with
the same initial letter sound?

sat   San

rock   rocket

Nid   num

Pem   pop

28

Answers: s: **San** and **sat**; r: **rock** and **rocket**; n: **Nid** and **num** and p: **Pem** and **pop**.

Words that rhyme have the same sounds at the end. Can you match up these rhyming words?

rock

pat

go

lid

did

sat

sock

no

Reading With Your Little Bugs

Here are some tips to help you enjoy reading this book with your child.

1   Encourage your child to read the story to you, saying the sounds and putting them together to read the word.

2   If your child gets stuck on a word, show them how to break it down into sounds.

3   Have fun! You can make up silly voices for each of the characters and even act out the story together.

4   Remember to give your child lots of praise!

5   If your child is starting to feel tired or bored, put the book away and pick it up another day.

Have fun and enjoy reading my story together.

Mind-Boggling Phonics Glossary

Phonics often feels a bit confusing,
with lots of alien terms. This glossary
will help demystify Phonics!

blend to put individual sounds together to read a word, e.g. s-n-a-p blended together reads 'snap'.

CVC word a word spelled with a consonant, then a vowel, then a consonant, like 'sat' or 'tip'.

decode to put sounds and letters together to read a word correctly.

digraph two letters representing one sound, e.g. ck in 'kick'.

grapheme a letter or group of letters representing one sound, e.g. t, b, sh, ch, igh, ough (as in 'though').

phoneme a single unit of sound, e.g. the letter 't' represents just one sound and the letters 'sh' represent just one sound.

segment to split up a word into its individual phonemes in order to spell, e.g. the word 'cat' has three phonemes: /c/ /a/ /t/.

sight words or high-frequency words are words that appear most often in printed materials. They may not be decodable using phonics (or too advanced) but they are useful to learn separately by sight to develop fluency in reading.

tricky words are words that cannot be sounded out with phonics, such as 'the', 'was' and 'one'. Sometimes called exception words.

trigraph three letters representing one sound, e.g. igh in 'night'.

GET TO KNOW READING GEMS

Reading Gems is a series of books that has been written for children who are learning to read. The books have been created in consultation with a literacy specialist.

The books fit into five levels, with each level getting more challenging as a child's confidence and reading ability grows. The simple text and fun illustrations provide gradual, structured practice of reading. Most importantly, these books are good stories that are fun to read!

Phonics is for children who are learning their letters and sounds. Simple, engaging stories provide gentle phonics practice.

Level 1 is for children who are taking their first steps into reading. Story themes and subjects are familiar to young children, and there is lots of repetition to build reading confidence.

Level 2 is for children who have taken their first reading steps and are becoming readers. Story themes are still familiar but sentences are a bit longer, as children begin to tackle more challenging vocabulary.

Level 3 is for children who are developing as readers. Stories and subjects are varied, and more descriptive words are introduced.

Level 4 is for readers who are rapidly growing in reading confidence and independence. There is less repetition on the page, broader themes are explored and plot lines straddle multiple pages.

Phonics